LITTLE CRITTER'S
ADVENTURE STORYBOOK

BY MERCER MAYER

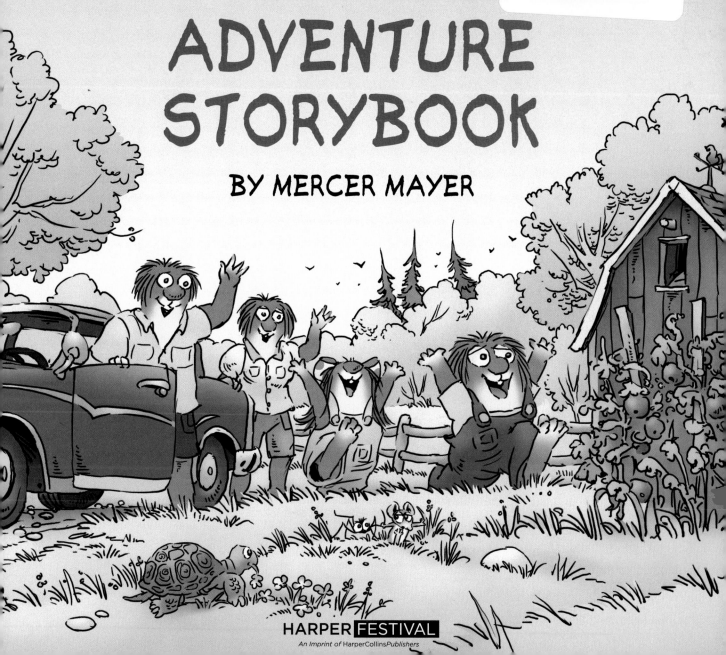

HARPER FESTIVAL
An Imprint of HarperCollins Publishers

TABLE OF CONTENTS

THE LOST
DINOSAUR BONE

BY MERCER MAYER

To Matilda Skiles,
Welcome to the World.
Glad You're Here!

Our class went on a field trip to the Museum of Natural History. I couldn't wait to see the dinosaurs. When I grow up, I'm going to be a dinosaur hunter.

But when we got to the museum, the dinosaur exhibit was closed.

So, we had to see the butterflies instead. The butterflies were fun, but I really wished we could see the dinosaurs.

Next, we went to the Rain Forest. There were lots
of trees with monkeys in them.

"Oooh! Oooh!" I said to the monkeys.

A guard came running over to see the monkeys, too, so I asked him about the dinosaurs. I found out that the exhibit was closed because a Triceratops bone was missing!

In the Hall of Gems and Minerals it was very dark, so we had to wear miner hats with lights on them. Tiger went looking for diamonds, but I was busy looking for the missing dinosaur bone. No luck!

After that, we went to the Planetarium, where the ceiling turned into a sky filled with stars.

We found out that the planet Mars is covered with dust and that the planet Saturn has rings around it.

I kept my eye out for the dinosaur bone, but I didn't see it.

On our way to see a meteorite, I asked Miss Kitty if I
could get a drink of water.

When I found the fountain, I also found something
else—the dinosaur exhibit! It had a big sign saying
EXHIBIT CLOSED.

I went closer and saw a Tyrannosaurus
rex. It was heading right for me!

I ran away as fast as I could . . .

. . . and found myself face-to-face with a Velociraptor. It had its mouth open wide so I could see all its sharp, pointy teeth.

The guard told me the exhibit was closed because of the missing dinosaur bone.

"I know," I said. "I've been looking for it everywhere."

On my way out, I took a wrong turn. That's when I saw something long and white sticking out from under the Ankylosaurus skeleton. It was the missing dinosaur bone!

I ran back to tell the guard.
He didn't believe me at first . . .

. . . but when I
showed the bone to
him, he gave me this
big smile.

Then I told Miss Kitty, and the guard took our whole class to the special place where the scientists who study dinosaur bones work.

"Thank you for solving the mystery of the missing Triceratops bone," the scientists told me.

The scientists took us on a tour of the dinosaur exhibit. They showed us a Stegosaurus skeleton they had found buried in a mountain.

"I'm going to be a dinosaur hunter when I grow up!" I said.

"You already are," answered the scientists.

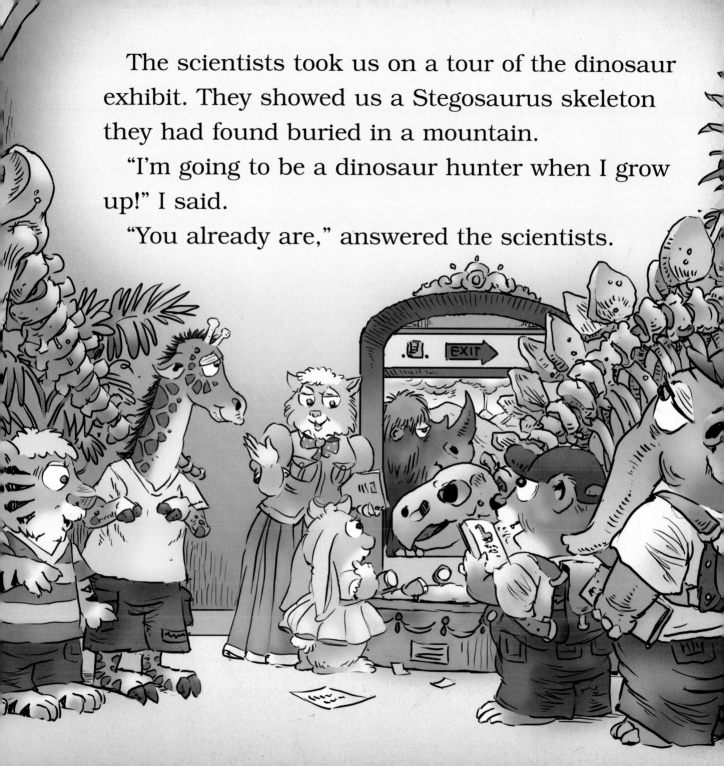

You know what I'm going to do tomorrow?
Dig for dinosaur bones in my backyard!

JUST A DAY
AT THE POND

BY MERCER MAYER

To the Elves . . .
Dianer, Bonnie, and Rita!

I went to Grandma and Grandpa's to spend a day at the pond. Little Sister came, too. Mom and Dad were going shopping. They would pick us up later.

Little Sister went with
Grandma to make a
picnic lunch.

I went to the shed to pick out some fishing poles with Grandpa.

Grandpa put a wagon on the big
tractor for us to ride to the pond. I
drove, but not by myself.

We picked a great picnic spot. Little Sister wanted to go swimming, but I wanted to go fishing first.

I put a worm on the hook.
It was slimy.

I waited and waited for
a fish to bite my worm.

Suddenly . . .

. . . something was tugging on my fishing line. It was pulling me into the water.

"Help, Grandpa," I yelled.

Then the line broke.
I thought it was a shark,
but it was just a turtle.

Little Sister was swimming with Grandma.
"Teach me to swim, Grandpa," I said.

I ran to the waters edge, but
then I changed my mind.

I wanted to catch frogs instead.

I found a bunch of frogs.

I snuck up on them very quietly.

But the frogs were too fast.

I was all muddy.

Grandma had to pour a million
buckets of water over me.
"Oh, look!" she said. "Little Sister
is swimming so well with Grandpa."

I could swim if I wanted to, but
I decided to explore instead. I
found a good hiking stick.

I found a hole in the ground. I stuck my hiking stick into it. Something made a buzzing sound.

It was ground bees. I
ran as fast as I could.

Grandpa came and got me.
We jumped into the pond and
the bees went away.

I was floating. I
kicked my feet . . .

. . . and paddled my arms
as fast as I could. I was
swimming with Grandpa.

I swam with Grandma
and Little Sister, too.

"Wow, Grandpa," I said.
"I guess I can swim after all."

JUST A
LITTLE MUSIC

BY MERCER MAYER

To Zeb,
Our Drummer Exemplar!

One day my family went to town to watch a parade. Many people were there to see the marching band. The music was very loud.

Little Sister had to cover her ears. I liked all the different instruments.

I said to Dad, "I want to play music, too."

When the parade ended, Dad and I walked to the music store to look at instruments. I hoped that Dad would let me get one.

While we were at the music store, Mom and my sister went shopping for clothes and other stuff.

The store was filled with so many instruments.
"Wow, Dad!" I said. "I like the tuba."
But the tuba was just too heavy.

The flute was too squeaky.

The trombone was too long.

The guitar had too many strings.

But the drum was just right.

"That's it!" I said to Dad. "I will be a drummer."

Dad signed me up for lessons. I couldn't wait to start playing my drum.

I played it during the car ride home. It was a long ride, so I had a lot of time to play.

I played my drum before bed until
Mom finally said, "Go to sleep now!"

I played my drum before breakfast
until Mom made me go to school.

After school, I invited my friend over
to see my drum.

But when I went to get it, it was not in my room.

I searched and searched, but I couldn't find my drum anywhere.

"Mom," I called. "My drum is missing!"

Mom asked Little Sister, "Did you do something with your brother's drum?"

"I hid it in my room," said Little Sister.
"He never stops playing, and it is too noisy!"

"Go and get it now!" Mom said.

The next day, I had my first lesson
with the music teacher.

I'm a very good musician! I'm so good
my teacher let me try playing his drums.

Soon I will play my drum in a rock-and-roll band. I can't wait for my family and friends to see me play.

They will be so proud of me.

But maybe before I play at my big
rock-and-roll concert, I will have just
a few more lessons.